Selfie

SANDY HORSLEY

CLICK!

for Thomas

Raintree is an imprint of Capstone Global Library Limited, a company
incorporated in England and Wales having its registered office at 264 Banbury
Road, Oxford, OX2 7DY – Registered company number: 6695582

www.raintree.co.uk
myorders@raintree.co.uk

ISBN 978 1 3982 0199 6

Designed by Brann Garvey
Originated by Capstone Global Library Ltd

British Library Cataloguing in Publication Data
A full catalogue record for this book is available from the British Library.

Printed and bound in India

Selfie

SANDY HORSLEY

Sylvie LOVES selfies.

#sylvie

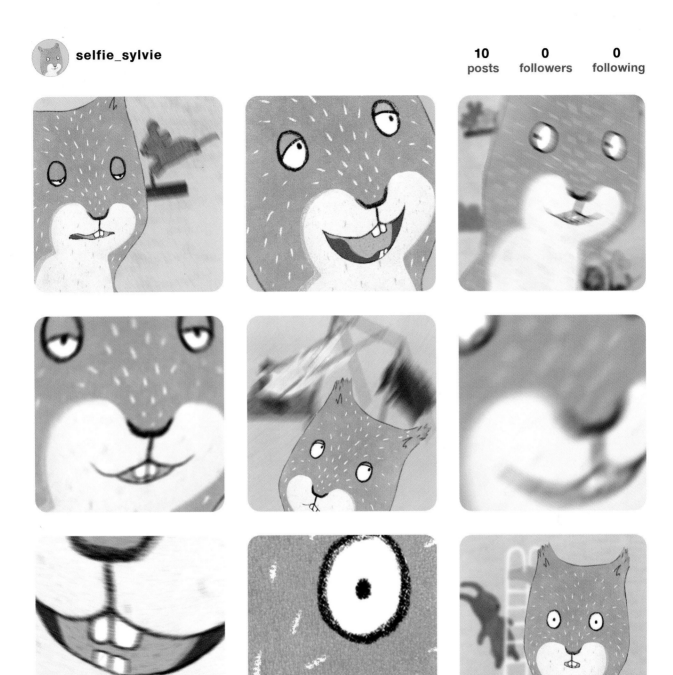

selfie_sylvie   #selfie   #squirrel   #funwithphotos

#cheesygrin   #notquitegotthehangofit   #itsallaboutme

Sylvie loves selfies a bit TOO much.

She misses out on all the fun.

One space left on the seesaw, Sylvie!

Come for a spin, Sylvie!

She's always looking for the
next photo opportunity.

And she **NEVER** looks
where she's going.

Sylvie's search for selfies takes her right into the deep dark woods.

Toadstool Turn

#toadstool

Popular Playground

Butterfly Bend

#butterfly #bird

Bird Boulevard

#followthatbird

N W E S

Grassy
Grove

#strangelights

#birdsong

Fairy
Forest

DEEP

DARK

WOODS

#whatsthatglowing?

Sylvie's friends
are worried.

Has anyone
seen Sylvie?

#alittlebitlost

#haveyouseenthissquirrel?

Meanwhile . . .

 selfie_sylvie

21
posts   **1**
followers   **0**
following

#whatcoulditbe?

#likefairylights

#magical

#twinklinglights

selfie_sylvie Look what I found!

#fireflies #socute #newfriends

After her scary adventure in the deep dark woods,
Sylvie realizes all the fun has been happening . . .

#imissedwhatwasundermynose   #whatasillysquirreliam

. . . right in front of her!

Instead of getting lost in selfies, Sylvie now gets lost in lots of fun and laughter with her friends.

#bestfriends

#i ♥ myfriends

#foreverfriends

#lostinthemoment
#noweveryoneisinthepicture

#theendofthisstory
#butjustthebeginningoflotsmorefun!